HELLO, I'm THEA!

I'm *Geronimo Stilton*'s sister. As I'm sure you know from my brother's bestselling novels, I'm a special correspondent for *The Rodent's Gazette*, Mouse Island's most famous newspaper. Unlike my 'fraidy mouse brother, I absolutely adore traveling, having adventures, and meeting rodents from all around the world!

The adventure I want to tell you about begins at Mouseford Academy, the school I went to when I was a young mouseling. I had such a great experience there as a student that I came back to teach a journalism class.

When I returned as a grown mouse, I met five really special students: Colette, Nicky, Pamela, Paulina, and Violet. You could hardly imagine five more different mouselings, but they became great friends right away. And they liked me so much that they decided to name their group after me: the Thea Sisters! I was so touched by that, I decided to write about their adventures. So turn the page to read a fabumouse adventure about the

★ THEA SISTERS! ★

Colette

She has a passion for clothing and style, especially anything pink. When she grows up, she wants to be a fashion editor.

Paulina

Cheerful and kind, she loves traveling and meeting rodents from all over the world. She has a magic touch when it comes to technology.

Violet

She's the bookworm of the group, and she loves learning. She enjoys classical music and dreams of becoming a famous violinist.

THE THEA SISTERS

Nicky

She comes from Australia and is very enthusiastic about sports and nature. She loves being outside and is always ready to get up and go!

Pamela

She is a great mechanic: Give her a screwdriver and she'll fix anything! She loves pizza, which she eats every day, and she loves to cook.

Do you want to help the Thea Sisters in this new adventure? It's not hard — just follow the clues!

When you see this magnifying glass, pay attention: It means there's an important clue on the page. Each time one appears, we'll review the clues so we don't miss anything.

**ARE YOU READY?
A NEW MYSTERY AWAITS!**

Geronimo Stilton

Thea Stilton
THE PHANTOM
OF THE ORCHESTRA

Scholastic Inc.

Copyright © 2016 by Edizioni Piemme S.p.A., Palazzo Mondadori, Via Mondadori 1, 20090 Segrate, Italy. International Rights © Atlantyca S.p.A. English translation © 2019 by Atlantyca S.p.A.

The publisher does not have any control over and does not assume any responsibility for author or third-party websites or their content.

GERONIMO STILTON and THEA STILTON names, characters, and related indicia are copyright, trademark, and exclusive license of Atlantyca S.p.A. All rights reserved. The moral right of the author has been asserted. Based on an original idea by Elisabetta Dami. geronimostilton.com.

Published by Scholastic Inc., *Publishers since 1920,* 557 Broadway, New York, NY 10012. SCHOLASTIC and associated logos are trademarks and/or registered trademarks of Scholastic Inc.

Stilton is the name of a famous English cheese. It is a registered trademark of the Stilton Cheese Makers' Association. For more information, go to stiltoncheese.com.

No part of this publication may be reproduced, stored in a retrieval system, or transmitted in any form or by any means, electronic, mechanical, photocopying, recording, or otherwise, without written permission of the copyright holder. For information regarding permission, please contact: Atlantyca S.p.A., Via Leopardi 8, 20123 Milan, Italy; e-mail foreignrights@atlantyca.it, atlantyca.com.

This book is a work of fiction. Names, characters, places, and incidents are either the product of the author's imagination or are used fictitiously, and any resemblance to actual persons, living or dead, business establishments, events, or locales is entirely coincidental.

ISBN 978-1-338-30615-6

Text by Thea Stilton
Original title *Due cuori a Londra*
Cover by Valeria Brambilla and Flavio Ferron
Illustrations by Barbara Pellizzari, Chiara Balleello, Antonio Campo, and Alessandro Muscillo
Graphics by Giovanna Ferraris and Chiara Cebraro

Special thanks to AnnMarie Anderson
Translated by Andrea Schaffer
Interior design by Becky James

10 9 8 7 6 5 4 3 2 1   19 20 21 22 23

Printed in the U.S.A.   40
First printing 2019

WHEN YOU LEAST EXPECT IT

The **bell** rang to end classes for the day at Mouseford Academy. Mice spilled out of their classrooms into the hallway, filling it with cheerful squeaks.

"Do you want to watch a M O V I E together tonight?" Pamela asked her friends the Thea Sisters. "There's a new action film I've been wanting to see."

Colette replied, "After a long week of schoolwork, I think I'm in the

mood for something light and **fun**."

"What do you think, Violet?" Pamela asked. But Violet wasn't paying any attention to her friends. Instead, she was STARING at her cell phone.

"Violet?" Pamela asked again.

"Huh?" Violet replied, glancing around in confusion. "What?"

"Let me guess," Paulina teased. "You were checking your email again."

Violet smiled, a little embarrassed.

"Yes, that's exactly what I was doing!" she replied.

A few weeks ago, the music teacher told Violet that an orchestra in London had an opening for a violinist. They were performing a new musical version of William Shakespeare's tragedy Romeo and Juliet. Violet decided to audition, and she had been waiting eagerly for the results. Unfortunately, she hadn't heard a thing.

"I don't think I got the **part**." Violet sighed. "I'm sure they chose someone with more **experience** playing in a big orchestra. Still, I can't stop checking my email!"

"Well, you know what they say." Nicky comforted her friend. "Things have a way of happening when you least expect them. Maybe you should try to just stop **thinking** about it for now."

Violet agreed to give it a try, and the friends headed back to their dorm. A few hours later, the mouselets were watching a movie when

Hmmm...

things **unfolded** exactly as Nicky had guessed they would.

Buzz! Buzz!

"Do you hear that?" Paulina asked, **LOOKING** around.

"It's Violet's cell phone!" Colette exclaimed, pointing to the table.

They all **LOOKED** at Violet. Their friend was nestled in the cushions, fast asleep.

Paulina glanced at the screen.

"Well, it seems our sleeping beauty just received a text from a theater in London," she told her friends. "It says: CONGRATULATIONS!"

"She got the part!" Nicky whispered excitedly.

"We have to tell her right away," Pamela said.

"Or we could **surprise** her!" Colette suggested with a big smile.

When Violet woke up from her nap a short while later, she was alone. Her friends had disappeared! But there was a note on the pillow next to her. It read:

We have AMAZING news! But you'll have to solve this puzzle to find out what it is. Go to the library and find a special book on the third shelf in the first section.

Still a little tired from her nap and confused by the note, Violet went to the **LIBRARY** and went to the first section of bookshelves. She quickly found a book on the third shelf that **STOOD OUT** from the others.

"*Romeo and Juliet*!" Violet exclaimed. She opened the book and found another **CLUE** inside.

You might already have solved the mystery, but don't stop now! Go to Pamela and Colette's room. The surprise is waiting for you there!

Violet hurried to Colette and Pamela's room and took a **deep breath** before she knocked.

"Come in!" a voice called.

When she opened the door, she found her friends standing there holding a big sign with words that were MUSIC to her ears.

"The orchestra finally contacted you," Pamela explained. "You were chosen!"

Violet's eyes filled with **happy** tears.

"I can't believe it!" she squeaked.

"Well, **BELIEVE** it!" Colette said happily. "Your **adventure** is about to begin."

READY TO GO!

Violet contacted the orchestra in London immediately and got all the **details**: Rehearsals with the rest of the musicians were to begin in London the following week.

With just a few days to prepare, Violet was determined to spend as much time as she could with her **friends** before her trip. Unfortunately, though, ever since Violet's exciting news, her friends had been very **busy**!

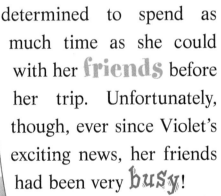

Every time Violet suggested they do something together, the four mouselets had other plans. But Violet had no intention of giving up.

"How about we go get a **snack** when you're all done studying?" she suggested one afternoon.

"I wish I could," Colette said, "but I have to **clean out** my closet."

"And I have to go for a **run**," Nicky added. "I can't skip my workout!"

"I really need to study," Pamela mumbled without **LOOKING UP** from her book.

"Sorry, Violet," Paulina said apologetically. "But I told Tanja I would try to fix a problem she's having with her **computer**."

"Okay," Violet replied with a *sigh*. "Maybe next time."

Maybe next time . . .

Over the next few days, Violet tried **again** and **again** to get the other Thea Sisters to spend some time with her before she left for **London**, but it was never a good time. On the day before her trip, Violet finally worked up the **COURAGE** to confront her friends.

"What's going on? Why don't you want to spend time with me before I leave?" she asked **sadly**.

Colette, Pamela, Nicky, and Paulina watched as Violet's eyes filled with TEARS. They quickly realized it was time to tell Violet what was REALLY going on.

"Please don't cry, Violet! The truth is that we really **want** to come with you!" Colette admitted, hugging her friend.

"These last few days, we've been trying to get all our work done so we could make the trip," Paulina explained. "We wanted to **surprise** you."

"Y-y-you're coming with me?" Violet stammered.

"Yup!" Pamela nodded happily. "We're all going to **London**!"

"That's **amazing**!" Violet exclaimed.

"You truly are the best friends!"

With the other Thea Sisters by her side, Violet knew this **adventure** would be even more MAGICAL!

WELCOME TO LONDON!

Before they left, the Thea Sisters read through many tourist guides, and they knew London was often gray and rainy. So they were pleasantly **surprised** to find the sun SHINING when they arrived.

"What a beautiful day to spend walking around and *exploring* the city!" Nicky exclaimed happily.

The five friends hailed one of London's **famous** black cabs and made their way to the bed and breakfast.

The **mouselets** were staying in a small bed and breakfast a stone's throw away from Piccadilly Circus, one of the most famouse areas in **London**.

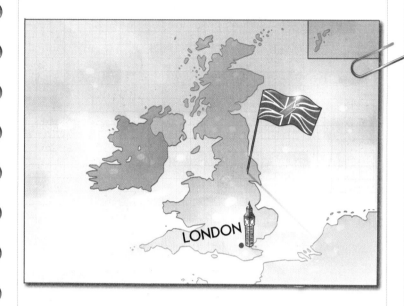

LONDON

The capital of the United Kingdom, London is a multicultural metropolis and about 30 percent of its residents are born in other nations. London's most famous monuments include Buckingham Palace — the residence of the royal family — and the spectacular Tower Bridge. This structure spans the River Thames, and the roadway opens up to allow large ships to pass. The iconic Big Ben — the bell inside the clock tower at the Palace of Westminster — is another famous London landmark.

"What a beautiful place!" Colette said, climbing onto one of the bunk beds in the room the friends were sharing.

"And it has a great view," Paulina added as she opened the window and stepped out onto a small BALCONY.

"Yes, just LOOK at the city!" Nicky exclaimed. "Are you all ready to go out?"

The friends dropped off their things and headed outside right away. First they got on

one of London's **RED** double-decker buses. Their *destination*: Buckingham Palace! There they watched the **famouse** Changing of the Guard ceremony, during which the guards on duty are replaced by those on the next shift. After that, they walked to the London Eye, the **ENORMOUSE** Ferris wheel on the bank of the River Thames. From the top, the Thea Sisters could see the entire city!

They also visited Westminster Abbey, the **GOTHIC** church where almost every British **king** or queen has been crowned.

"I could really use a **snack**," Pamela said as they left the abbey. "All this sightseeing

has really made me **hungry**!"

The Thea Sisters headed to a restaurant and ordered "jacket potatoes" (a name for baked potatoes used in the UK!) served with various toppings. Then they shared a **delicious** sticky toffee pudding. This traditional British dessert isn't really pudding! It's a moist sponge cake made with dates and covered in a sweet caramel sauce.

When they returned to the bed and breakfast, a mouse stood just outside the entrance, studying a map of the city.

"Are you lost?" Pamela asked the stranger kindly. "We aren't from here, but maybe we can help you."

"I'm fine," the mouse replied, eyeing them suspiciously. Then Violet noticed that he was holding a **ViοLiη**.

She looked more closely and realized he had the musical score to *Romeo and Juliet* tucked under one arm. He must have been a member of the **orchestra**, too!

"Are you here for the orchestra rehearsals?" she asked. "So am I! My name is **Violet**, and these are my friends."

"I'm Sarat," he answered quickly. "Yes, I'm in the orchestra, and I'm already **late**."

With that, he **hurried** away.

Violet hoped that the other members of the orchestra would be more **friendly**!

A WARM WELCOME

An hour later, Violet found herself at the theater, which was inside an ancient *Victorian~era* palace not far from where she and her friends were staying. Violet's **heart** was in her throat as she stood in front of the building looking at posters advertising the show 𝕽𝖔𝖒𝖊𝖔 𝖆𝖓𝖉 𝕵𝖚𝖑𝖎𝖊𝖙.

Suddenly, she realized just how SPECIAL this moment was. Her **DREAM** of playing in a professional orchestra was about to come TRUE!

"Are you ready?"

Nicky asked, squeezing her friend's paw encouragingly.

"Yes!" Violet exclaimed happily as she

entered the building. Inside, the managers and the crew were already starting the rehearsal.

A mouse approached Violet.

"Hi, you must be Violet," he said, smiling and shaking her paw. "I recognize you from your audition. My name is Richard. I am the conductor!"

After that WARM welcome, Violet introduced Richard to her friends and explained that they had decided to join her on her trip.

"It will be a *pleasure* to have you here," he said. "Now follow me and I'll introduce you to the rest of the team."

The friends hurried after him and quickly met the director, Louise, and her assistant, John.

Then they met Will and Mary, the two

young actors who were playing **Romeo** and *Juliet*. Finally, Richard introduced Violet to the rest of the **orchestra**.

"We've met before," Violet said to Sarat. "We're actually staying at the same bed and breakfast."

"Oh, great," Richard replied. "Sarat was also Selected during auditions."

Then the conductor turned to the rest of the orchestra.

"Let's all give Violet and Sarat a warm welcome," he said with a friendly smile.

Colette couldn't help but notice that Sarat seemed **bored** by everything Richard had said so far. But she kept it to herself because she didn't want to ruin Violet's moment.

"Now, there's only one more mouse for you to meet," Richard said as he LOOKED around the theater.

"WHAT ARE YOU DOING?" someone yelled suddenly from the back of the theater.

"Why haven't you started rehearsing yet? We only have a few days before we hit the stage."

Richard nodded toward a mouse walking down the aisle.

Let's get started!

"That's Paul Bennet, our **producer**," he told Violet. "It seems to me that he doesn't really need an INTRODUCTION."

A ROMANTIC STORY

After her initial introduction to the orchestra and cast, Violet and her friends had some free **TIME** before the first full rehearsal. So they headed back to the bed and breakfast to read **Romeo and Juliet**.

"This is such a romantic story." Colette sighed, clutching the book to her chest.

"It's a classic," Nicky agreed. "It's hard to believe it was written at the

HISTORY

Romeo and Juliet is a tragedy by the playwright William Shakespeare. It is the story of a couple who fall hopelessly in love but cannot be together because they are the children of rival families.

end of the sixteenth century, yet everyone still thinks it's **amazing** today!"

"Have you read the passage where Romeo and Juliet meet for the first time?" Paulina asked. "It's my absolute favorite."

While her friends looked for the right page, Violet kept an eye on the clock. She had to get back to the theater soon for her first rehearsal with the actors.

"I think we should head back," she told her friends. "I don't want to be **LATE**."

"You're right!" Colette said. "I can't wait to hear the music. I'm so curious about how it all comes together."

As soon as the five friends walked into the theater, they could feel the excitement. The actors and the musicians were reviewing scripts and scores and waiting for the official start of the rehearsal.

Violet settled into her place in the **orchestra** while Paulina, Colette, Pamela, and Nicky took seats in the audience so that they could observe the rehearsal without disturbing anyone.

"Is it just me, or is Paul Bennet looking at us?" Pamela asked, trying to move her mouth as little as possible.

"You're right," Nicky agreed. "Now he's coming toward us. I hope we aren't doing something **wrong**."

"Good morning!" Paul greeted them warmly a moment later. "I see that you've come to watch your friend **rehearse**. However, I'm afraid you won't be able to see much.

"We're having a small problem with the **LIGHTING SYSTEM**. The lights aren't **bright** enough, but the crew doesn't have the time to go buy the correct cables. We just can't afford to lose them in the middle of a rehearsal. I'm sure you can **UNDERSTAND**."

"Of course," Nicky replied. Then she had an idea. "Would it help if we were to go pick up the **CABLES** for you?"

"Yes, that would be perfect!" Paul answered immediately. Then he handed Paulina a slip of paper with an address.

"They'll know what to give you," he said. Then he quickly **scurried** off.

"That was a little **strange**," Colette admitted as she and her friends headed for the exit. "He seemed to know we would offer to go."

"I know what you mean," Nicky agreed. "I wonder if this errand is an excuse to get us out of the **THEATER**."

"Maybe," Paulina replied as she plugged

the **address** from the paper into the GPS on her **phone**. "Or maybe he just needed some extra help and he was hoping we'd volunteer. We'd better get going . . . This place is pretty *far away*!

A BiG miSTAKE

After sending the mouselets to the other side of the city to pick up the **CABLES**, the producer wouldn't stop asking for their help! A few days later, while the rehearsals continued, Paul sent Colette, Pamela, Nicky, and Paulina to pick up lunch from his *favorite* restaurant. Unfortunately, his directions were confusing, and the friends soon found themselves in an unfamiliar part of **London**.

"Do you think we're supposed to go THIS way or THAT way?" Pamela asked. She tilted her head to one side to study the **MAP** she held in her paws.

"We came from the right, so maybe we should go left . . ." Nicky replied.

"Are you sure we didn't come from the **left**?" Paulina asked, disheartened. "I remember passing this library earlier. Without the exact address

to plug into my **phone**, we're never going to find the place."

"Okay, then," Colette said, sighing. "Let's just go back. This By the River restaurant is IMPOSSIBLE to find!"

"Wait!" Paulina said, pointing to a mouselet who had just passed them. She was holding a tote bag with the words By the River printed on it. "Maybe she can help us!"

The Thea Sisters rushed after the mouse to ask for directions. A few minutes later, they finally found the **restaurant**.

When they returned to the theater, the atmosphere was tense. A few of the actors were standing on the stage wearing costumes while Paul **SHOUTED** at a ratlet who had a lost expression on his snout.

"This is a disaster!" the producer cried as he paced back and forth across the stage. "They simply cannot go on stage dressed like this!"

The Thea Sisters looked closer and realized that the costumes were at least two sizes **TOO BIG**.

"I am so glad you're back," Violet whispered to her friends. "Paul will **calm down** a bit after he's had his lunch."

Violet took advantage of the lunch break to fill in her **friends** on what happened.

"The costumes came in the wrong size," she explained. "Paul is FURIOUS, and he's taking it out on Matt, the costume designer. But Matt says it isn't his fault. Paul even called the tailors to see what happened. Here they come now."

"**There you are!**" Paul exclaimed as the

Oooh!
This is a disaster!
I'm sorry . . .
Please calm down.
He's so angry!

two tailors walked in. "Now we can figure this all out. Why are these costumes the wrong size?"

The tailors exchanged a puzzled look. "We made the clothes based on the information we received," the tailor named Meg explained.

"Actually, we had to do extra work to get these done in time. We had already finished the costumes when Matt called to explain that the MEASUREMENTS he gave us had been incorrect. We had to start over from the BEGINNING!"

"Me?" Matt said, incredulous. "I never called to change anything."

"Now these costumes are unusable!" Paul huffed.

"There must have been some sort of a misunderstanding," Paulina said. She couldn't remain silent any longer. "I don't think this is Matt's fault. There must be some other explanation."

Meg nodded. "We don't know what really happened," she said.

"I'm not sure who to believe," Paul said irritably as he continued to pace the stage. "In any case, this error has cost us a lot of time and work. Now we have to pay to have these fixed!"

"I don't think Matt is lying," Paulina whispered to her friends when everything calmed down.

What should we do?

"But the tailors also seem ʃincere," Colette added. "What do you think is going on?"

"I'm not sure," Paulina said. "But it's very strange.

How strange . . .

From now on, the five of us must keep our eyes and ears open!"

mAKiNG NEW FRiENDS

After Paul's **outburst**, the rehearsal resumed. But the atmosphere was anything but relaxed!

Everyone was tense and anxious because of the mistake that was made with the costumes. While the actors waited to rehearse their next scene, the orchestra continued to practice songs from the show. Despite the difficult situation, the Thea Sisters really enjoyed watching Violet play with a professional **orchestra**. They were so **proud** of her!

Mary, the actress playing *Juliet*, approached the four friends.

"It was very nice of you to step in and

defend Matt," she told Paulina. "Sometimes Paul can be a little RUDE. But I believe he behaves that way because he really **cares** a lot about the show."

"Just like the rest of us," said Will, the actor playing **Romeo**.

Colette smiled at him. "You're going to amaze everyone in the audience," she said. "From what we've seen in rehearsals, the entire cast is very talented!"

The two actors seemed pleased with the compliment. They sat down and spent a large part of the break with the Thea Sisters, chatting. Mary and Will were both kind and social, and they seemed genuinely interested in getting to know the mouselets better.

"It must be **interesting** to study at a great school like Mouseford Academy!" Mary said. "I would love to come visit one day."

"You'd be most welcome," Colette said.

"We can show you some P I C T U R E S of the school and of Whale Island," Nicky added. "I have some on my phone."

She patted her pocket, looking for her phone. Then she remembered that she had left it in her **BACKPACK** in the dressing room.

"Let me go get it!" she said.

As she walked through the deserted hallways, she recognized Paul's voice.

"Louise!" he was squeaking with the director. "How could we have let that happen? This is a very **SERIOUS** mistake. Fixing them will be very expensive, and you know we can't afford that."

"I am sure it was just a **misunderstanding**," she replied, trying to reassure him. "We'll fix everything."

"I hope so!" Paul replied. "Otherwise I might have to stop rehearsals and shut down the entire show!"

Nicky kept walking toward the dressing room, hoping that everything would work out for the best. She liked to stay positive,

but the idea that the show might be canceled made her **heart** heavy. Violet was working so hard, and Nicky knew how much this opportunity meant to her friend!

EXPLORING LONDON!

Fortunately, rehearsals continued without any **unexpected** events for the next two days.

Colette, Paulina, Nicky, and Pamela were always in the first row, supporting Violet.

"It sounds like you've been a part of this **orchestra** your whole life!" Colette said with a smile.

"Yes, the group plays so **beautifully** together," Nicky agreed. "And the cast and musicians are all so friendly."

She gestured to Mary and Will, who were waving to them from the stage.

"Well, **MOST** of them are," Paulina added. "It seems there are a few who want **NOTHING** to do with us!"

Paulina pointed at Sarat. He was seated next to Violet and they were sharing a MUSIC STAND, but he barely even glanced her way. He acted the same way whenever he was around the other Thea Sisters: He seemed **annoyed** to have them around.

The mouselets decided to talk to Mary about it after rehearsal that day.

"Sarat?" she said, confused. "But he's very nice! I've spoken to him before. Maybe he's a bit **shy**. You just have to get to know him."

"I have an

idea!" Paulina said. "If you two are already friends, maybe he will accept your *invitation* to spend time with us after rehearsal tomorrow. That way we can all have a chance to get to know him."

Mary liked the idea. Once rehearsal was over, she approached him.

"Hi, Sarat!" she called. "Would you like to come for a ride around **London** with us after rehearsal tomorrow?"

At first Sarat remained silent. Then he **blushed** and nodded.

"See?" Paulina squeaked happily. "It worked!"

The Thea Sisters were

Hi, Sarat!

excited. Since Mary was from **London**, they could see the most famouse places in the city, but she could also show them more out-of-the-way corners of the city that weren't usually visited by tourists.

The next day, the group headed out as soon as rehearsal ended.

"This is the British Museum!" Mary said as they pulled up in front of a large building. "It's one of the biggest museums in the city — and the WORLD!"

As they explored the museum, Sarat kept to himself at first. But as time passed, he relaxed and became friendlier.

"If you're not too tired, I can take you to the most beautiful place in the entire city," Mary said once they had left the museum.

"London is so fantastic, it's impossible to get tired," Nicky replied. "Does anyone need a snack? I brought some **energy bars**!"

Sarat took one happily.

"You five are very good friends to one another," he admitted to Violet. "I can tell by how you take care of each other."

"It's true," Violet replied with a nod. "We're **INSEPARABLE**!"

A few minutes later, Mary stopped and

This is the British Museum!

gestured to the trees and lawns all around her.

"**Welcome to Hyde Park!**" she announced. The Thea Sisters saw that they were in the middle of an immense **PARK**. It was filled with tourists as well as Londoners who had come to spend a little time in **nature**.

Wow . . .

It's wonderful!

Yes, it is!

I love Hyde Park!

The group found a quiet corner, and Mary and Will put down a blanket so they could enjoy a **tasty** picnic.

"It's so beautiful, I could stay here **forever**."

Pamela sighed as she lay

on the grass next to Colette.

"This has been a great day," Violet said, happy to have succeeded in making friends with Sarat. "I'm sad that it's almost over."

"Well, it's not over yet," Mary replied. "You can't end a day of sightseeing in **London** without a cup of

REAL ENGLISH TEA!"

A TEATIME MYSTERY

After a relaxing break in the park, the friends headed to an English tearoom. The tables were covered with trays of pastries and small sandwiches, and the aroma of tea filled the air. Mary explained to her friends that **five o'clock tea** is a kind of ritual for British mice.

"Five o'clock tea started in the nineteenth century with Queen Victoria," Mary explained while sipping a cup of fragrant EARL GREY tea. "We British have done our best to keep the **tradition** going!"

"Well, I approve!" Pamela remarked as she bit into a tiny butter-and-cucumber sandwich.

"We should take the **tradition** back

It's a tradition!

I love it!

It's delicious, right?

Mmm!

with us to Mouseford Academy," Colette joked.

"That is a great idea!" Pamela agreed. "Now, if you'll excuse me, I'm going to get a slice of cake."

She stood up and headed for the buffet, where she was overwhelmed by the **delicious-looking** assortment of cakes, scones, and biscuits. As she was deciding which one to try, a mouse in a great hurry bumped into her.

"**OOPS!**" he squeaked.

Pamela looked up to see that it was the director's assistant, John.

"John?" Pamela replied. "Hello!"

But he acted as though he had never seen her before. A split second later, he disappeared through the front door.

Pamela noticed he had dropped some **FLYERS**, and she quickly picked them up and went back to the table to rejoin her friends.

"You didn't get dessert," Colette said in surprise when Pam returned without any cake.

Nicky looked curiously at the flyers. "And

DID JOHN REALLY NOT RECOGNIZE PAMELA, OR WAS HE JUST PRETENDING?

why are you holding flyers announcing the grand opening of a new **MULTIPLEX CINEMA**?"

"It's a long story," Pamela replied, a puzzled expression on her snout. "And I don't think the director's assistant, John, likes me very much."

ANOTHER MISTAKE

Before coming to London, Colette thought she wouldn't enjoy exploring a new city unless it was sunny and warm outside. But in **London** it was different. Even though it rained often, the sky was gray, and the streets were usually foggy, the weather gave the city character.

The **cloudy** sky in the morning didn't make Colette want to burrow back under the covers. Instead, she wanted to jump out of bed and enjoy every corner of the city!

"Wake up, mouselets!" Colette squeaked happily as she opened the curtains. "**London's** calling!"

After a breakfast of porridge and fruit, the Thea Sisters put on their **raincoats** and rain boots and rushed out to the theater. The rehearsals were going **smoothly**, and Paul was still asking the mouselets to help with small jobs during rehearsals.

"The messenger who was bringing us the final

FOOD

Porridge is a mixture of grains or cereal boiled in water or milk and typically served for breakfast. Fruit is often added to make the dish sweeter.

scripts couldn't make it," the producer said as soon as the friends arrived at the theater.

Pamela nodded AGReeaBLy.

"No problem," she said. "We can go get them. It will give us

a chance to explore a new area of the city!"

So the mouselets headed to the copy shop, using the opportunity to take a walk across one of London's most famous landmarks: **TOWER BRIDGE**.

With the rain 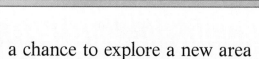beating

down on their open umbrellas, Colette, Paulina, Pamela, and Nicky stopped for a moment in the middle of the bridge and enjoyed the **VIEW** of the river. Once they had picked

up the scripts, they quickly returned to the theater. They were back just in time to hear **Violet** and the rest of the orchestra rehearsing one of the most beautiful songs in the show. As they watched their friend, the other Thea Sisters realized Violet and

Sarat seemed much more in tune than they had been before.

Both mice were smiling brightly as they played.

"There you are!" Paul said when he saw the mouselets. He took the bag with the scripts eagerly. "As soon as the orchestra

is finished rehearsing we will begin with the actors."

Paul distributed the scripts, and Will opened his and began to FLIP through it.

It's all wrong!

"Hey!" Will exclaimed suddenly. "My script has the wrong lines!"

Unfortunately, his wasn't the only script that wasn't quite right.

"Mine is wrong, too!" Mary echoed immediately. One by one all the actors agreed. The scripts were **unusable**.

"Mouselets, what's going on?" Violet asked her friends. "How is it possible that all the scripts are **wrong**?"

"I don't know," Paulina said, frowning. "We only did what was asked of us. We went to the copy shop and picked up the scripts.

They were already printed when we got there, so our guess as to what happened is as good as anyone else's."

Pamela noticed Paul was walking toward them, an ANGRY look on his snout.

What a disaster!

"Something tells me we should probably come up with a guess quickly, though," she whispered to her friends.

LOOKING FOR PROOF

Paul quickly caught up with the mouselets and began **questioning** them.

"What happened to those scripts?" he asked angrily. "Is this your idea of a **JOKE**?"

The four friends were about to reply when John stepped in to help.

"Please, Paul, stay **calm**," he said. "We don't know what happened here or who is responsible. But we certainly can't blame these mice. After all, they were doing you a **favor** by picking up the scripts."

Colette, Nicky, Paulina, and Pamela were **touched** by the way the director's assistant defended them. Pamela was especially surprised given the way John had acted at the tearoom.

"I don't see who else could have made such an **ERROR**," Paul replied. Then he turned to the mouselets with a stern look. "You four may not be responsible, but we've had too many ISSUES in this theater lately. I would prefer if you no longer came to **WATCH** rehearsals."

It wasn't our fault...

Who else could it have been?

We're very sorry...

Oh no!

"But why?" Violet asked, astonished. "My **friends** have always been kind and helpful, and they aren't at fault!"

The producer didn't reply. Instead, he walked away while everyone else watched, **STUNNED**.

"I'm very **sorry**," John said, approaching the Thea Sisters. "You didn't deserve to be accused like that."

"That's kind of you to say," Colette replied, smiling. "But we understand why Paul is

ISN'T IT STRANGE THAT JOHN DIDN'T RECOGNIZE PAM AT THE TEAROOM, BUT HE CAME TO HER DEFENSE RIGHT AWAY IN THE THEATER?

upset. He's worked hard for this show and he wants to make sure there are no more setbacks."

The mouselets said good-bye to Violet and left the theater.

"You don't want to go back to the bed and breakfast, do you?" Paulina asked, **imagining** that her friends were thinking the same thing she was.

"Of course not!" Nicky said.

"We know we aren't responsible for what happened to the scripts," Paulina continued.

"But we don't know what really happened, or why," Colette agreed.

"We'll just have to find out, then!" Nicky exclaimed.

"I agree," Pamela said. "But where should we start LOOKING?"

Paulina gave her friends a look.

"Exactly where it all started," she said. "We have to go back to the **copy shop**."

We have to figure out what happened!

Yes!

We can do it!

TWO EMAILS, ONE SENDER?

Having read dozens of mystery books, Paulina had learned that every **Mystery**, even the most complex and intricate, has a very simple explanation at the end.

Though it's not always easy to find the explanation, Paulina was sure of one thing: If she and her friends had the patience to put together the pieces of the **puzzle**, they would soon figure out what had happened.

The four friends hurried back to the **copy shop**, where they were greeted by the owner, Victoria.

"Hello again!" she exclaimed upon seeing Paulina, Colette, Pamela, and Nicky back in the shop. "What are you doing back? Were the scripts okay?"

"Actually, there was a **PROBLEM**," Nicky explained. "We think the file you printed from was **incorrect**."

"You should talk to my son, **ALBERT**," Victoria replied, pointing to an open door. "He's in the back."

The **THEA SISTERS** thanked her and headed to the back room, hoping Albert would have some answers.

When they **EXPLAINED** the problem

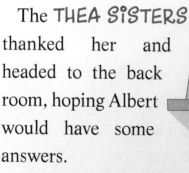

Ask my son, Albert!

to him, the young mouse seemed very sorry and surprised.

"I don't know what could have happened," he said. "I simply printed the file Paul sent me."

"That's what I thought." Pamela sighed. "Thank you anyway for your help."

"**WAIT!**" Albert shouted suddenly as they were almost out the door. "Now that I think about it, I didn't receive just one file. I received two different emails with two different attachments."

Albert showed the mouselets the email on the computer.

Paulina read the email out loud: *"Good morning, Albert. Attached are new versions of the scripts. Please print these and not the previous ones. Thanks so much."*

"But why would Paul send the wrong

script?" Nicky asked, confused. "That doesn't make sense."

"Maybe he was distracted," Pamela suggested.

"The email is from Paul's email address," Albert said. "That's why I didn't call to confirm."

"It's not your fault," Colette assured him. "But do you think you could print the first file for us now?"

"As soon as the scripts are ready, we'll have to take them straight to the theater," Pamela explained. "The actors are already behind on their rehearsals."

As Albert started the print job, Paulina had a sudden realization.

"Paul sent the correct version of the file to Albert," she told her friends. "But then someone else sent another file. The same thing happened with the costumes. In both cases, someone messed things up by calling or emailing to give **contradictory** information. Isn't that ODD?"

Pamela nodded.

"Yes, it's strange," she agreed. "But it's still possible Paul sent the wrong file because he was distracted."

"Actually, I don't think Paul sent both files," Paulina explained. "When I looked at Albert's computer, I noticed that the two emails seem to be from two **different** addresses. The first one is really from Paul: The address is PAULBENNETPRODUCTIONS@THEATERMAIL.COM.

But the other is from PAULBENNETPRODUCTIONS@ THEATERVISION.COM. At first glance they look the same, but they aren't!"

"The scripts are ready!" Albert announced. "I did them as quickly as I could."

"Thank you!" Paulina said gratefully. "But we have one more favor to ask you," Paulina said. "Could I use your computer for a moment to do a little bit of research on the emails you received?"

"Sure." Albert smiled. "Anything to help solve the Mystery!"

Paulina sat down at the computer while

CLUE!

THE TWO EMAILS CAME FROM TWO DIFFERENT ADDRESSES. WHO SENT THE SECOND EMAIL PRETENDING TO BE PAUL? THE FIRST EMAIL CAME FROM: PAULBENNETPRODUCTIONS@THEATERMAIL.COM THE SECOND EMAIL CAME FROM: PAULBENNETPRODUCTIONS@THEATERVISION.COM

Pamela, Colette, and Nicky hurried back to the theater with the correct scripts. Once they **arrived**, they saw Violet sitting in a corner of the orchestra pit, deep in conversation with Sarat during a break from the rehearsal.

"Hey!" Violet **greeted** them warmly. But

We have the correct scripts!

Here they are!

Ohh!

then she glanced around nervously. "What are you doing back here?"

"We brought these!" Pamela said, showing her the new **scripts**. The mouselets told Violet and Sarat what had happened and what they had DISCOVERED at the copy shop.

"Paulina is doing some research," Colette explained. "As soon as she has more information, she'll be back."

"Let's not waste any more time," Nicky chimed in. "Why don't you get these **scripts** to the actors so the rehearsal can continue?"

"I can't wait to see this," Violet said with a smile.

"See **WHAT**?" Colette asked.

"How Paul reacts when he sees what you've done for him, and then apologizes for kicking you out!" Violet replied, laughing.

ANOTHER POSSIBILITY

When the **THEA SISTERS** returned to the theater with the correct scripts, they brought some **peace** and **calm** back to the rehearsals. Louise, the director, didn't know how to thank the mice.

Finally!

"You really **saved** us," she squeaked happily.

Even grumpy Paul couldn't help but **smile** when thanking the mouselets.

Pamela took the opportunity to quickly explain what they had learned at the copy shop, and to ask him some questions.

"Did you send the second email to Albert at the copy shop?" she asked him.

Paul shook his head decisively. "Definitely not."

Pamela **LOOKED** at her friends. "I don't know about you, but I am very confused," she said.

At that moment, Louise's voice **BOOMED** through the theater.

"Come on, everyone, let's get started!" she announced.

The actors in the first scene took their places, ready to start. Mary was playing Juliet, and an actor named Susan was the nurse. But just as Susan was about to deliver a line . . . **BAM**!

A piece of the famouse balcony Juliet appears on in one of the most important scenes in the play came **crashing** down, barely missing Susan!

"Are you okay?" Pamela asked in alarm as she hurried onto the stage.

"Yes, thank you," Susan replied, but she was clearly shaken.

"How did this happen?" Paul asked in dismay. "Why is something always going wrong?"

"Don't lose your TEMPER," Louise said, trying to calm him. "I'll call the set designer and ask him to fix this right away. Everything will be okay, you'll see."

Paul took a deep breath.

"I hope you're right," he muttered, shaking his snout. "If one more thing goes wrong, I'll have to consider CANCELING the show."

Then he stormed out of the rehearsal.

As soon as he was gone, the mouselets approached Louise to try to cheer her up.

At Paul's threat to shut down the show, her expression had changed. The cheerful smile she always wore disappeared.

"Paul was just very ANGRY," Nicky reassured her. "That's the only reason he said those things."

"I think so, too," Colette agreed. "The show is really wonderful! Surely everyone will do all they can to get it onto the stage."

"Thank you," Louise said. "You mouselets are very kind. But the situation is more complex."

"Go on," Pamela said. "Tell us about it."

"Unfortunately, the theater is going through a rough time," Louise told them. "Some of the recent shows here haven't gone very well, and Paul has put everything into this one. If Romeo and Juliet doesn't have a successful opening night, I'm afraid the theater may have to close down permanently."

As she spoke her eyes filled with TEARS.

"I've worked in this theater for my entire career, and the thought of having to say good-bye is very **painful**," Louise explained.

"I'm so sorry," Colette said. "I don't know for sure what will happen with the show, but I do know one thing: My friends and I will do everything we can to help solve this Mystery!"

LET THE INVESTIGATION BEGIN!

After confiding in the Thea Sisters, the director returned to her work. She ran

Let's continue . . .

lines with the actors while everyone waited for the set to be fixed. Louise was a true **professional** and, after watching her work, it was clear that she had a lot of experience.

The mouselets were very impressed by the kind and **confident** way she directed the actors. She reassured them and encouraged them to improve.

"I can't believe they may have to

shut down the theater forever," Pamela said. "It can't close — it's just not right!"

The mouselets were quiet as they each reflected on the unusual events that had occurred so far during their stay in London.

"Unless . . ." Colette said suddenly. "Unless the reason these things keep happening is because someone is trying to get the theater to close down!"

"But why?" Nicky asked. "Who would want to do that?"

"I have no idea," Colette replied, sighing. "It's just one theory."

"Let's hope Paulina can find something INTERESTING during her research," Pamela said. "In the meantime, we can't leave everything to her. We should start doing some investigating ourselves!"

"Pamela is right," Violet said. "I care way

too much about this show to let it fail."

"Okay, so let's start investigating," Pamela agreed.

"Count me in," came a *familiar* voice behind them. It was Sarat! "I want to do

Let's start investigating!

We can help!

Let's do it!

something, too. Sorry, but I couldn't help but **OVERHEAR** your conversation, and I want to help."

"Of course!" Nicky replied with a smile. "We can use all of the help we can get!"

Count me in!

"Absolutely!" Violet said happily. Even though the thought of the theater closing still made her sad, she smiled. Sarat had turned out to be much more like her than she had thought. He was just a little shy, and sometimes that made him seem unfriendly. Luckily, Violet knew now that he was a REAL friend.

A SIMPLE ACCIDENT?

Colette, Pamela, Violet, Nicky, and Sarat decided to question Peter, the **head technician**, first. He had worked in the theater for DECADES, and he had helped create and build hundreds of set designs. Peter was on the stage fixing Juliet's BALCONY when they found him.

"Can we ask you some questions?" Pamela asked.

"Sure," Peter replied, putting away his hammer in his **toolbox**. Then he pointed to the balcony. "I'm almost done here. It's not as beautiful as it once was — unfortunately you can still see the crack. But at least now no one will get **hurt**."

"What do you think happened here?" Sarat

asked, hoping for an answer that would help make sense of everything.

Peter shook his head. "I don't know," he admitted. "The piece that came off had been well attached to the main structure. But maybe you should ask John. I saw him go on stage just before it happened. Maybe he noticed something I didn't."

The mice followed Peter's advice. But John's answer wasn't very helpful, either.

"It was an **accident**," John said with a shrug. "Sometimes accidents happen without any reason. I don't know what else to tell you."

Then he abruptly walked away.

"I hope everything goes smoothly from now on," Colette said.

But at that moment, someone began shouting loudly.

"NO. I WILL NOT ACT ON A STAGE THAT FALLS APART!"

The mice turned to find Susan, the actress who

It was just an accident...

Wait!

was playing Juliet's nurse, rushing toward the exit looking very **annoyed**.

"It doesn't sound like things are going very **smoothly**," Pamela said.

ONE CLUE LEADS TO THE NEXT

Violet, Pamela, Nicky, Colette, and Sarat quickly followed Susan to the theater exit. They were going to try to calm her down and convince her to stay.

"You got **scared**, which is completely normal," Violet said gently as she tried to reassure Susan. "But Peter fixed it and the balcony is **stronger** than ever."

"Yes, I guess you are right," Susan replied, still a little **shaken**. "I would hate to leave the show now, but it seems like everything is **falling apart**!"

"Would it help if we went back inside with you?" Violet asked Susan gently.

Susan nodded.

The group was just walking back toward the **stage** when the front door opened and Paulina came in.

"What's going on?" she

asked her friends. "What are you doing in the lobby?"

"There was another small setback," Colette explained as she glanced at Susan, who was walking to her dressing room with Violet. "But, fortunately, it seems like everything is under control."

Where have I heard that name?

"What about you?" Pamela asked Paulina. "Were you able to discover anything new?"

"Not much," Paulina admitted. "I searched on Albert's computer for hours, but I have only one clue. The strange email address belongs to a real estate company called VISION."

"So it's likely Paul really

didn't send the second email," Nicky concluded.

"Wait a **second** . . ." Sarat said suddenly. "I know Vision!"

"My father worked for them a few years ago," Sarat continued. "They develop shopping centers and multiplex cinemas."

Pamela was quiet for a moment as she thought about what Sarat had just said. Then she grabbed her **BACKPACK** and began to rummage through it.

"Here it is!" she squeaked as she pulled out the flyer that John had dropped in the tearoom. "I knew I hadn't thrown it away."

"Are you saying there's a link between **VISION** and this flyer?" Violet asked.

"I'm not sure," Pamela replied. "But the flyer mentions a multiplex cinema. Maybe we should ask John about it."

"Yes, that's a 𝕘𝕣𝕖𝕒𝕥 idea," Violet said.

Paulina took the flyer from her friend to get a closer 𝕃𝕆𝕆𝕂.

"It's 𝕝𝕦𝕔𝕜𝕪 you kept this," she told Pamela.

"Yes," Pamela agreed. "It's a good thing I always forget to 𝕔𝕝𝕖𝕒𝕟 𝕠𝕦𝕥 my bag!"

CLUES!

THE EMAIL ADDRESS USED TO SEND THE INCORRECT SCRIPT BELONGED TO A REAL ESTATE COMPANY THAT BUILDS MULTIPLEX CINEMAS, AND THE FLYER JOHN DROPPED AT THE TEAROOM IS FOR A NEW MULTIPLEX CINEMA IN LONDON. WAS IT JUST A COINCIDENCE, OR WERE THE TWO THINGS RELATED?

ONE LIE TOO MANY

The Thea Sisters and Sarat hoped talking to John would clear up some of their questions about the strange incidents of the last few days.

When they tried to get his attention, though, they realized he wasn't going to be very helpful.

"I'm too busy right now," he replied when they approached him. "I simply don't have time to chat."

But Pamela persisted.

"We just wanted to ask you one quick question," she explained. "Do you remember when we bumped into each other at the tearoom?"

John seemed **startled** by the question.

"Uh, yes . . . I remember," he mumbled. "But I was in a hurry to get back to the theater, just like I'm in a **hurry** now."

"Wait!" Pamela continued, showing him the flyer. "It will only take a moment. I just

wanted to ask you **ONE THING** about this."

But John didn't answer. Instead, he just walked away

I'm in a hurry!

quickly, leaving the Thea Sisters and Sarat even more **perplexed** than before.

"Didn't that seem very **strange** to you?" Nicky asked her friends. "He really didn't want to squeak with us."

"And the little bit he did tell us was a total **LIE**," Paulina added. "There was no rehearsal the afternoon we were at the tearoom, so it isn't true that he was *rushing* back here when he bumped into Pamela."

"It seems like John is *hiding* something," Nicky remarked.

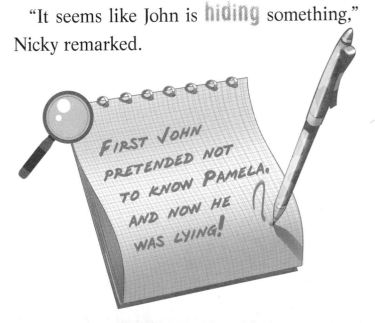

FIRST JOHN PRETENDED NOT TO KNOW PAMELA. AND NOW HE WAS LYING!

"Maybe we should tell Paul what we've **discovered**," Violet said.

The group found Paul talking to the conductor, Richard.

"We need to talk to you," Paulina told the producer. "We've discovered a few things about the incidents that have been happening here in the theater."

"This isn't a good time," Paul replied, **annoyed**. "I have to get rehearsal up and running as soon as possible."

"But this might help us all understand what's been going on," Paulina tried to explain.

"I'm sorry," Richard said. "But we're already running so *LATE*, we can't **WASTE** any more time."

Paulina didn't dare ARGUE. Instead, she turned back to her friends, unsure of what to do. If their suspicions were correct, the rehearsals wouldn't go on for much longer.

THE MISSING VIOLIN

The next morning, Pamela woke up early. It was a very **IMPORTANT** day — today was the dress rehearsal!

Pamela had a plan to **surprise** her friends with a special **treat**. The five of them had been so focused on trying to solve the **Mystery** of the strange mishaps at the theater that they hadn't been taking much time to themselves to have **fun**. Pamela quietly got dressed, grabbed her backpack, and *slipped* out of the room.

When she returned, she brought back **Five** pieces of carrot cake and **Five** cups of tea.

"Good morning, sisters!" she called out,

closing the door behind her. "Breakfast is ready!"

"What a lovely surprise," Violet said as she got out of bed and grabbed a cup of tea from her friend. "**This is the best way to start the day.**"

The five friends sat on the bed and ate the

wonderful cake Pamela had brought them. When they were finished with their delicious breakfast, they *rushed* to the theater.

When they walked in, everything seemed **under control**. Richard was talking to some of the musicians, Louise and John were giving directions to the actors, and Paul was running BACK and FORTH making sure that everything was okay and there wouldn't be any other trouble.

"Okay, mouselets, let's keep our eyes and ears open today," Paulina whispered.

"Pay attention to **JOHN**," Pamela said. "But let's not be obvious about it. We don't want him to know we're WATCHING him!"

The mouselets were determined not to let rehearsal be interrupted.

They watched carefully for any *suspicious* behavior from the assistant director.

"MUSICIANS, take your places!" Richard announced. "We'll get started in ten minutes."

Violet had just left her friends and taken her seat in the orchestra pit when a **SHOUT** rang out.

"What is it, Adam?" Richard asked, turning to the first violinist.

"My violin has **DISAPPEARED**!" the worried musician explained. "Last night I left it with the ***luthier*** * for a tune-up, and he said it would be ready and waiting for me in the orchestra pit today. But I've asked around, and no one knows where it is!"

"Let's try to stay calm," Pamela said. "For now, all we know is that the **VIOLIN** isn't where it should be. But we don't know for sure what happened."

But everyone had **DARK** and gloomy

---

* A luthier is someone who builds or repairs stringed instruments.

expressions on their snouts.

Pamela turned to her friends.

"I think it's time to start the investigation again!"

she said.

innocent until proven guilty

It was getting very close to showtime. It was too late to cancel or postpone the dress rehearsal. So, while the actors continued to review their parts, Colette, Pamela, Paulina, Violet, and Nicky offered to try to figure out where Adam's **Violin** had gone.

First, they headed straight to Mr. Smith's workshop. He was the **VIOLIN MAKER** who had tuned Adam's violin. The shop was just steps from the theater.

"Good morning, how can I help you?" the craftsman greeted the mice as soon as they entered his little shop.

"We were hoping to ask you some questions," Paulina explained. "Did you tune a **VioLin** for someone who plays in the **orchestra** at the theater next door?"

Mr. Smith nodded.

"I did," he replied. "The young mouse brought it to me **LAST NIGHT**. It's a beautiful instrument."

"Can you tell us where it is now?" Pamela asked.

"Didn't Adam ask that it be returned to the theater in time for the rehearsal this morning?"

"Yes, he did," the luthier replied. "But then someone from the orchestra came in **early** this morning to pick it up."

"Who?" Pamela asked, *intrigued*.

"I don't know his name," the luthier said. "But he was a tall mouse with brown hair and a green velvet jacket. He told me he

worked for the theater, and that the owner needed his violin back **right away** for a solo."

The **THEA SISTERS** looked at one another. Mr. Smith had just given the exact description of someone they knew very well!

"Thank you so much," Colette said. "You've been very **kind** and helpful!"

"Now we really have to get back to the theater," Paulina added as they ***rushed*** out the door. "Bye!"

"That description sounded just like John!" Nicky exclaimed. "But he couldn't have taken the **VioLin**."

"You're right," Violet agreed. "Louise told me this morning that she and John got to the theater at **Dawn** to get ready for today's dress rehearsal."

"But how can we be sure that John was

already at work when this **Mysterious** person went to the shop to pick up the violin?" Pamela asked, perplexed. "How can

He described John!

But how is that possible?

we be sure he was at the theater the whole time? Coud he have slipped out without anyone noticing?"

"There has to be an *explanation*, and it's up to us to figure it out!" Paulina concluded.

TOO MANY COINCIDENCES

When they returned to the theater after talking to Mr. Smith, the Thea Sisters found the same atmosphere they had left earlier.

"We can't wait any longer," Louise said. "We have to start the dress rehearsal NOW!"

"But how can we rehearse if Adam doesn't have a violin?" Richard pointed out. "He's first violin, and his part is very **important**! We can't do the show without him."

"Morale is very low around here," Violet remarked, sighing.

"Paul isn't even

THE DRESS REHEARSAL

During a dress rehearsal, the entire show is staged from the beginning to the end as if it is the real show!

YELLING at anyone," Pamela noted. "That's a bad sign!"

Indeed, Paul sat in a corner, his snout in his paws. He didn't seem very interested in finding a solution.

"We can get Adam a new violin!" Violet suggested. "Let's go back to Mr. Smith's

shop. I'm sure he can help us."

"I'll go with you," Sarat offered.

Back at the shop, the violin maker **welcomed** them, but he had unfortunate news.

"I'm afraid I don't have anything as good as the violin I tuned last night," he said apologetically. "But I know of another store that will certainly have something like it!"

Paulina typed the address into her tablet and frowned.

"That store is a bit *far*," she said. "But if we take the **Underground**, maybe we can get there and back quickly."

"We have to try!" exclaimed Pamela. So the group headed right for the Tube station.

When they arrived at their destination, Nicky pointed at a sign above a small shop with a **CELLO** in the window.

"There it is!" she said happily. "TURNER AND SONS!"

"You're right, Nicky!" Paulina confirmed, checking on the tablet.

"Good eye," Sarat added. "I wouldn't have spotted that little shop in the middle of all these BIG BUILDINGS!"

The friends scurried toward the music shop. Once inside, it was easy to find what they were looking for.

"Yes, I think I have a VIOLIN that would be just perfect," the shopkeeper said. "This is one of the last ones we have."

"One of the last ones?" Violet frowned.

"Yes, unfortunately my shop is about to close down," Mr. Turner explained. "The builders of the multiplex cinema next door want to demolish this building and put in a parking lot."

"**MULTIPLEX CINEMA?**" Pamela repeated softly. Could it be the same one as the one on John's flyer?

"That's right," the shopkeeper said, sighing sadly. Then he handed the mouselets the **VIOLIN**. "I've been working here for many, many years. Maybe it will be nice to retire a

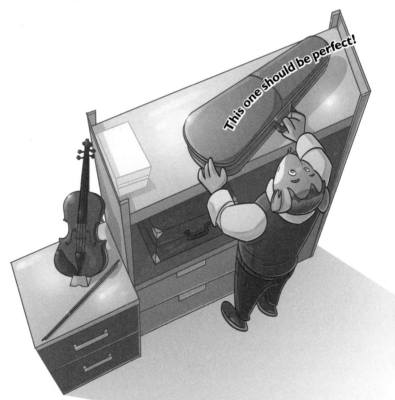

little earlier than I expected."

The friends left the shop with a new violin for Adam and headed to the Underground.

"Does it seem **strange** that we keep hearing about this **MULTIPLEX CINEMA**?" Pamela asked as she headed down the steps to the train.

"Yes, it does seem very ODD," Colette agreed. "I'm starting to think it can't be a coincidence."

SEEING DOUBLE

The Thea Sisters and Sarat emerged from the Underground and *RUSHED* back toward the theater with the new violin. Then, suddenly, Pamela stopped in her tracks.

"**LOOK!**" she said, pointing to a mouse waiting at a bus stop in front of a café. "Isn't that John?"

"Yes!" Colette replied. "But what's he doing out here instead of at the theater?"

"Let's go ask him!" Pamela said. She headed toward him, followed by the rest of the group.

"Hi, John!" Colette greeted him. "What are you doing here?"

"H-hi," he stammered. "I was just taking a break."

He glanced at his watch.

"Sorry," he mumbled, "but I have to be back in the theater in two minutes for rehearsal."

"Okay!" Paulina replied with a nod. "We'll see you *inside*."

She and her friends continued past John

and headed to the theater. But as she walked, Paulina had the sensation that something about John had been a bit off.

It was only when she got inside the theater that she realized what it had been — his WATCH!

"Hey!" she squeaked to her friends. "Did any of you NOTICE John's watch? He used to wear it on his LEFT wrist, as right-pawed mice do. But just now his watch was on his RIGHT wrist!"

At that moment Adam appeared.

"You're back!" he squeaked, a hopeful look on his snout. "Were you able to find me a new VIOLIN?"

"Yes, we were," Violet said happily as she gave him the instrument.

"Thank you," Richard told the mouselets gratefully. "You've really been a great help."

"Finally, the dress rehearsal can begin!" he cried happily.

At Richard's announcement, the musicians, actors, and technicians all began to scurry around excitedly, preparing to begin the rehearsal. Violet and Sarat moved to take their seats in the orchestra as the other performers tuned their instruments and went over their lines.

Pamela glanced across the theater and

We made it!

Here it is!

A violin! Thank you!

noticed something that left her *squeakless*.

"Look, there's John!" she cried, pointing to the front of the orchestra pit. John had **scripts** in his paws and he was deep in **conversation** with Louise. It certainly didn't seem like he had just arrived back at the theater. "How did he get down there so *quickly*?"

"I don't know," Paulina replied, confused. "And isn't he wearing his watch on his **LEFT** paw now?"

"But then **WHO** was that in front of the café a few minutes ago?" Nicky wondered, a **perplexed** look on her snout.

"I'm going to find out!" Pamela announced. Then she turned and **scurried** out of the theater. When she returned a little later, she

didn't have the answer her friends were hoping for. But she had gathered a little more information.

"There wasn't anyone standing in front of that café," she explained. "But when I went inside and talked to the *waitress*, she said he spends a lot of time there, talking on the **phone** and working on his computer."

"This keeps getting STRANGER!" Paulina said.

That evening after rehearsal, Colette, Nicky, Pamela, and Paulina were eager to update Violet and Sarat. The pair had been busy practicing all day, so they hadn't heard

It's impossible!

yet about the new clues.

"I don't have any idea what's going on," Violet admitted. "How can John work here at the **THEATER** and also spend so much time at the café, working on his laptop?"

THE FACTS

1. PAM BUMPED INTO JOHN AT THE TEAROOM, BUT HE HADN'T RECOGNIZED HER.

2. A FEW DAYS LATER, JOHN WAS VERY FRIENDLY TOWARD PAM AND THE OTHER THEA SISTERS.

3. THE EMAIL FROM PAUL TURNED OUT TO BE FROM A COMPANY BUILDING A MULTIPLEX CINEMA.

4. JOHN DIDN'T SEEM TO REMEMBER MEETING PAM AT THE TEAROOM.

5. THE MOUSE WHO PICKED UP ADAM'S VIOLIN AT THE REPAIR SHOP LOOKED LIKE JOHN, BUT JOHN HAD BEEN WORKING IN THE THEATER AT THAT TIME.

"Unless there are **two** of him, I don't see how it's possible, either!" Pamela said, shaking her head.

As she heard those words, everything CLICKED into place for Paulina. Suddenly, she understood **everything**!

"That's it, Pamela!" Paulina exclaimed. "The only way John can be in two places at the same time is if **he has a twin brother!**"

DOUBLE TROUBLE

The more the friends thought about it, the more EVERYTHING made sense. Well, almost everything.

"That explains why he didn't recognize me when we met at the tearoom," Pamela realized. "It wasn't John that day, but his twin!"

"There's still one thing I don't understand, though," Violet remarked. "What's the link with the MULTIPLEX CINEMA we keep hearing about?"

"I have an idea as to how we can figure out the rest of the pieces to this puzzle and expose John and his MYsterlous twin," Paulina said.

Then she quickly explained her idea to

Sarat and her friends. Once everyone had agreed on the plan, the Thea Sisters headed back to their bed and breakfast to get some rest.

The next day was the first performance of **Romeo and Juliet**. The Thea Sisters headed to

the theater early, **excited** and ready to put their plan into action. They couldn't wait to finally solve the **Mystery**.

"Sisters, we're *so close* to figuring this out!" Paulina reminded her friends once they were gathered just outside the theater. "Let's go over what we have to do."

"Nicky and I will come up with an excuse to draw Paul and Louise to the theater's entrance," Colette began.

"That means you, Paul, and Louise will be ready to WELCOME me, Paulina, and John's twin when we enter the building," Pamela continued. "It won't be easy to convince him to follow us, but we'll figure it out."

"At that point, Sarat and I will join you with the **REAL JOHN**!" Violet concluded.

"Let's do this!" the mouselets squeaked. Then they split up and got into their positions.

Colette, Violet, and Nicky *entered* the theater while Paulina and Pamela headed for the café, hoping John's twin was there.

"It's him!" Paulina said. She pointed to a mouse at a table near the window. He was drinking juice and working on a laptop.

"Great!" Pamela said. "I have an idea." She entered the café and approached the mouse at the table.

"Hi, John!" she said, greeting him **warmly**. "I was hoping to find you **HERE**!"

"H-hi," John's **twin** stammered, looking a bit nervous.

"I need your help **RIGHT NOW**!" Pamela explained. "There's been a **problem** with the programs for the show."

"I—I—I . . . really . . ." The mouse hesitated.

"I promise it will only take **Five Minutes**," Paulina added, reaching for his paw. "We left the programs in the hallway back at the theater."

For a moment, it seemed there was **No way** the mouse was going to follow her to the theater and risk bumping into the real John. But suddenly he stood up.

"All right," he replied. "But first I have to make a *phone call*."

Afraid he was about to call John to **WARN** him, Pamela put her arm around John's twin as if she was giving him a **friendly** hug. Then she pulled him toward the exit.

"You can do that later," she said. "This is IMPORTANT! We really have to *hurry*. I promise it will only take a moment. You'll see!"

From there, everything went exactly as PLANNED. A few minutes later, Pamela, Paulina, and the mysterious twin found themselves **snout-to-snout** with Louise and Paul, who were there because of something Colette and Nicky had told them.

"John!" the director exclaimed. "What are you doing here? Weren't you just behind the curtain?"

Finding himself in a difficult situation, the twin did exactly what the Thea Sisters had hoped he would do. He LIED and pretended to be John.

"Uh . . . yes, I was," he said quickly. "I just stepped out for a moment to make a phone call."

As if on cue, Violet, Sarat, and the real John came through the door a moment later.

"Tom!" John exclaimed, seeing his twin.

"What are you **DOING** here? I told you not to come here for any reason!"

Louise and Paul were so confused by the situation they didn't seem to know what to do. But finally Louise squeaked.

"I think you both have some EXPLAINING to do," she said, looking from John to Tom and back again.

"Yes, more explaining than you can imagine!" Paulina added.

ALL THE PIECES FIT

At first the brothers tried to play things off as a big **misunderstanding**. But as their story grew more confusing, they were forced to admit the truth.

"You two are responsible for all the **mishaps** around the theater, aren't you?" Paulina asked firmly.

"No, no, no," Tom replied. "You have it all **wrong**." He was clearly caught, but he didn't want to **give up**.

But, suddenly, John gave himself up.

"No, you're exactly **right**," he admitted. John glanced at his brother and then continued. "Tom, they've figured it out. I don't want to **LIE** anymore."

"So, you were the one who called the tailors and gave them the **wrong** measurements?" Louise asked John in shock. "And you **sabotaged** the set?"

"He had the **wrong** scripts printed and he stole the violin, too," Paul added, though he didn't seem angry. Instead, he looked crushed at the **realization** that his friend had been responsible for everything. "But **WHY** would you do all of this?"

Why did you do it?

"I think I have an idea," Pamela said, reaching into her pocket. She pulled out the flyer she had **saved** for days now. "It has to do with this, **RIGHT**?" she asked.

At that point, Tom gave up as well.

"I'm responsible for **everything**," he admitted. "I wanted this theater to **SHUT DOWN** permanently, and I convinced John to help me make the show go bust."

"But what would you have to gain from shutting down the show?" Paul asked, scratching his head. "I just don't **UNDERSTAND**."

"If this theater closed, Tom's real estate company, Vision, could buy the land and build another **MULTIPLEX CINEMA**," Paulina guessed.

"Yes, you're right," Tom admitted with a smile. He didn't seem to **regret** anything!

"I agreed to help him," John admitted sadly. "I am so sorry. I'm just as guilty as he is."

Tom and John's confessions clarified **everything**. Finally, all the pieces of the puzzle fit together perfectly. Still, not one mouse thought there was anything to CELEBRATE.

A TEAM THAT DOESN'T QUIT!

The musicians and **actors** had realized that Louise, Paul, John, Violet, and Sarat were missing, and they filed into the lobby to see what was going on.

The Thea Sisters filled everyone in on what John and Tom had done.

"You risked hurting me in order to open a movie theater?" Susan asked in shock.

"No, that's not true!" John exclaimed. "I **honestly** didn't know the balcony was going to **break**!"

"What about Adam's **VioLin**?" Mary asked.

"We have it," John replied quickly. "We'll give it back!"

"I don't want to hear any more," Paul said sadly. "I want you both to leave the theater **immediately**."

"Yes," Louise agreed. "We never want to see you again. And we'll be speaking to the press about Vision and the way they handle business!"

The two brothers knew there was nothing they could do at that moment to improve things, so they left quickly and without **arguing**. For a while, everyone in the theater stood in shocked silence, unable to move or squeak.

"I'm sorry all this drama has wasted so much of our rehearsal time," Paul told everyone. "I'm afraid the show just won't be as good as we had HoPeD."

"We only have a **few hours** before we have to go on stage," Louise said, looking worried.

Colette looked around and could see that everyone was feeling down. She knew she and her friends had to **help**!

"Come on, everyone!" Colette squeaked. "Snouts up! You can do this!"

"That's right!" Nicky agreed. "You can't give up now! You've worked **TOO HARD** to get to this point."

"Yes!" Paul agreed, suddenly *inspired*.

"You mice are a TEAM, and teams **don't quit.**
Let's get back onstage and do this.

The show must go on!"

A NEW BEGINNING

The whole crew quickly got back to work with new **enthusiasm**. They wanted everything to be ready for OPENING NiGhT!

Without her assistant director, Louise was far **busier** than anyone else. But the Thea Sisters were happy to step in to help as best they could. In the end, like all the moving parts of one big machine, the team got it done in time. Soon they found themselves taking their places. They were ready for the curtains to open!

Colette, Paulina, Pamela, and Nicky sat in the front row, waiting **eagerly** for the show to begin. They had seen it take shape and had helped solve the **Mystery** that had threatened to shut down the show —

and the theater — for good. Now they were excited to see how everyone's hard work had **paid off**!

"I can't wait for the show to start!" Colette squeaked.

"Me, too!" Nicky agreed. "But I think there's someone even more excited than we are."

The four friends watched as **Violet** took

How beautiful!

I can't wait!

her seat in the orchestra and awaited the curtain call. She looked very *elegant*, but they knew she was also a little nervous. Still, she was smiling BRIGHTLY, happy that her dream of playing with a professional orchestra was about to come true!

A few moments later, the curtains parted and the orchestra began to play the opening notes. The actors took their places on the stage, and the tragic story of Romeo and Juliet was soon underway!

A few hours later when the curtain closed to end the show, the audience ERUPTED in applause. The show had been a GReat SUCCeSS!

Everyone who had worked on the show gathered **backstage** to celebrate their first performance.

"Quiet please!" Paul squeaked from the

front of the room. "The opening night performance of *Romeo and Juliet* was magnificent. You all worked so hard to make this show happen. Thanks to everyone, the theater will remain **OPEN**!"

GOOD-BYE, LONDON!

"Does everyone have all their **things**?" Paulina asked as she and her friends shut the door behind them for the last time.

"Yes, and I have the plane tickets, too!" Nicky assured her.

"I brought extra **snacks** for the trip," Pamela added.

A few days had passed since the opening of the show, and Colette, Pamela, Paulina, and Nicky were reluctantly leaving Violet behind in London.

They had to return to their classes at **MOUSEFORD ACADEMY**. Meanwhile, Violet had received special permission to spend two more weeks in London performing.

Leaving the bed and breakfast that had become like their second home, the Thea Sisters headed for the airport. Sarat had graciously offered to give them a RIDE. It was a quiet trip as the friends thought about the exciting experience they had just had in London.

"I guess it's time to go," Colette said when they arrived at their gate. "We are going to count down the days until you come back."

"It's always hard to say good-bye, even if we know we will see you again soon," Paulina said, hugging Violet.

"And I'll see you all soon, too!" Sarat announced. "I'm looking forward to visiting Mouseford Academy and experiencing all the things you've been telling me about this week."

Colette, Pamela, Nicky, and Paulina said one last good-bye before **boarding** their plane. They were sad to leave their friend behind, but they knew the next two weeks

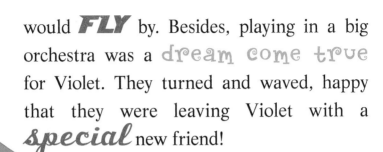

would *FLY* by. Besides, playing in a big orchestra was a dream come true for Violet. They turned and waved, happy that they were leaving Violet with a *special* new friend!

Bye!

See you soon!

Don't miss any of these exciting Thea Sisters adventures!

Thea Stilton and the Dragon's Code

Thea Stilton and the Mountain of Fire

Thea Stilton and the Ghost of the Shipwreck

Thea Stilton and the Secret City

Thea Stilton and the Mystery in Paris

Thea Stilton and the Cherry Blossom Adventure

Thea Stilton and the Star Castaways

Thea Stilton: Big Trouble in the Big Apple

Thea Stilton and the Ice Treasure

Thea Stilton and the Secret of the Old Castle

Thea Stilton and the Blue Scarab Hunt

Thea Stilton and the Prince's Emerald

Thea Stilton and the Mystery on the Orient Express

Thea Stilton and the Dancing Shadows

Thea Stilton and the Legend of the Fire Flowers

Thea Stilton and the Spanish Dance Mission

Thea Stilton and the Journey to the Lion's Den

Thea Stilton and the Great Tulip Heist

Thea Stilton and the Chocolate Sabotage

Thea Stilton and the Missing Myth

Thea Stilton and the Lost Letters

Thea Stilton and the Tropical Treasure

Thea Stilton and the Hollywood Hoax

Thea Stilton and the Madagascar Madness

Thea Stilton and the Frozen Fiasco

Thea Stilton and the Venice Masquerade

Thea Stilton and the Niagara Splash

Thea Stilton and the Riddle of the Ruins

Thea Stilton and the Phantom of the Orchestra

And check out my fabumouse special editions!

THEA STILTON: THE JOURNEY TO ATLANTIS

THEA STILTON: THE SECRET OF THE FAIRIES

THEA STILTON: THE SECRET OF THE SNOW

THEA STILTON: THE CLOUD CASTLE

THEA STILTON: THE TREASURE OF THE SEA

THEA STILTON: THE LAND OF FLOWERS

THEA STILTON: THE SECRET OF THE CRYSTAL FAIRIES

Don't miss a single fabumouse adventure!

Up Next:

Visit Geronimo in every universe!

Spacemice

Geronimo Stiltonix and his crew are out of this world!

Cavemice

Geronimo Stiltonoot, an ancient ancestor, is friends with the dinosaurs in the Stone Age!

Micekings

Geronimo Stiltonord lives amongst the dragons in the ancient far north!

Join me and my friends as we travel through time in these very special editions!

THE JOURNEY THROUGH TIME

BACK IN TIME:
THE SECOND JOURNEY THROUGH TIME

THE RACE AGAINST TIME:
THE THIRD JOURNEY THROUGH TIME

LOST IN TIME:
THE FOURTH JOURNEY THROUGH TIME

NO TIME TO LOSE:
THE FIFTH JOURNEY THROUGH TIME

THE TEST OF TIME:
THE SIXTH JOURNEY THROUGH TIME

Don't miss any of my adventures in the Kingdom of Fantasy!

THE KINGDOM OF FANTASY

THE QUEST FOR PARADISE:
THE RETURN TO THE KINGDOM OF FANTASY

THE AMAZING VOYAGE:
THE THIRD ADVENTURE IN THE KINGDOM OF FANTASY

THE DRAGON PROPHECY:
THE FOURTH ADVENTURE IN THE KINGDOM OF FANTASY

THE VOLCANO OF FIRE:
THE FIFTH ADVENTURE IN THE KINGDOM OF FANTASY

THE SEARCH FOR TREASURE:
THE SIXTH ADVENTURE IN THE KINGDOM OF FANTASY

THE ENCHANTED CHARMS:
THE SEVENTH ADVENTURE IN THE KINGDOM OF FANTASY

THE PHOENIX OF DESTINY:
AN EPIC KINGDOM OF FANTASY ADVENTURE

THE HOUR OF MAGIC:
THE EIGHTH ADVENTURE IN THE KINGDOM OF FANTASY

THE WIZARD'S WAND:
THE NINTH ADVENTURE IN THE KINGDOM OF FANTASY

THE SHIP OF SECRETS:
THE TENTH ADVENTURE IN THE KINGDOM OF FANTASY

THE DRAGON OF FORTUNE:
AN EPIC KINGDOM OF FANTASY ADVENTURE

THE GUARDIAN OF THE REALM:
THE ELEVENTH ADVENTURE IN THE KINGDOM OF FANTASY

THE ISLAND OF DRAGONS:
THE TWELFTH ADVENTURE IN THE KINGDOM OF FANTASY

THANKS FOR READING, AND GOOD-BYE UNTIL OUR NEXT ADVENTURE!

TheaSisters